STO

FRIEND
OF ACPL

VICTORIA CHESS AND EDWARD GOREY

Fletcher and Zenobia

ILLUSTRATED BY VICTORIA CHESS

Meredith Press   New York

First edition

Library of Congress Catalog Card Number: 67-22803
Manufactured in the United States of America   Meredith Press

To George

Once there was a cat named Fletcher who lived in the largest and tallest tree for miles around. He had run up it in a moment of thoughtless abandon, and ever since had been unable to get down again.

The tree also harbored a vast, brass-bound leather trunk. Fletcher often wondered how *it* had got there.

It contained all sorts of things, including a collection of hats for all occasions. Alas, not one single one had arisen as long as Fletcher had been in the tree.

In fact, there was almost nothing to do but walk back and forth along the branches or watch the clouds going past in the sky.

One day, however, Fletcher was rummaging about in the depths of the trunk when he came across a papier-mâché egg larger than himself. It was covered with orange roses on a violet ground, and was rather dusty; a band of tarnished gold-filigree paper went round its middle.

"Ho!" said Fletcher. "I never saw *that* before."

With some difficulty he heaved the egg from the trunk and wedged it in the fork of a branch. As he was attacking it with a duster, he noticed a label pasted to it near the top. The writing was much faded, but he decided that it read: *For the attic (unwanted by Mabel).*

"Is there someone there?" said a faint voice from inside the egg.

"Is there someone *there?*" said Fletcher, who was startled.

"Only Echo," said the voice, sadly.

"No, my name is Fletcher."

"Mine is Zenobia," said the voice. "How do you do?"

"How do you do?" said Fletcher.

"Not too well," said Zenobia. "My feet are asleep. Do you think you might open the egg and let me out?"

"Of course. I'll go and get an axe."

There was a muffled shriek. "That won't be necessary. It comes apart in the middle. Under the gold paper. Twist!"

After twisting in the wrong direction until he was quite short of breath, Fletcher realized his mistake and at last succeeded in removing the top.

Tottering slightly (for her feet were all pins and needles) but elegant withal, an old-fashioned doll stepped from the bottom half of the egg. She was dressed in mauve velvet, and though her face was plain, the ribbons on her gown and the flowers on her hat were stylish indeed—not to mention her buttons.

"How do you do again," they both said together and ceremoniously shook hands.

"What were you doing inside that egg?" asked Fletcher.

"Mine is a long, sad story," said Zenobia, wriggling first one foot and then the other to restore the circulation. "Fortunately, I can remember almost none of it."

"Who was Mabel?"

"An unfeeling child. You will not be surprised to learn she had fat wrists." Zenobia shuddered. "But let us not speak of her."

She looked around her with puzzled interest.

"We are in a tree," said Fletcher.

"A perfect place for a sunny summer afternoon," said Zenobia. "Where do you live otherwise?"

Fletcher explained there wasn't any otherwise.

"I don't think I should much care for it here on a rainy night in winter. Besides, the great world is out there below."

Fletcher sighed; he had nearly forgotten it entirely.

"We shall have to find a way to get down," said Zenobia. She opened her parasol and peered at the result. "No, that won't do."

She sat down and dangled her legs disconsolately. "Oh, dearie me."

"We could have a party," said Fletcher to cheer her up, uttering the first thing that came into his head.

"Why not?" said Zenobia, uttering the first thing that came into hers.

So they set to, and by the time the sun had gone down, Zenobia had baked a lemon cake with five layers, which she covered with raspberry icing and walnuts and decorated with green and blue candles ("Perhaps it's one of our birthdays," she said), and Fletcher had made four quarts of peach ice cream in the freezer and three gallons of pineapple and strawberry punch in the silver punch bowl.

By the time the moon had risen, they had blown up what seemed like at least several hundred balloons, although really there were only twenty-seven.

As they were getting their breaths back, Fletcher thought of the hats. "This *is* an occasion, isn't it?" he asked.

"Indeed it is," said Zenobia.

Fletcher went and got the hats from the trunk. "Which ones ought we to wear?"

Zenobia surveyed the hats, and frowned. "I'm afraid I'm not quite certain."

"Then let's wear the ones we like best."

So after much trying-on and taking-off of hats, exchanging of opinions, and changing of minds, Zenobia at last chose one for being in a gondola on the Grand Canal of Venice, and Fletcher picked one to wear while being presented to a maharajah in the course of an elephant hunt.

A little while later the party was in full swing and Zenobia was teaching Fletcher how to reverse while waltzing.

"Now bring your left foot," said Zenobia, "around in back of—"

"What was that?" said Fletcher.

"No, your *left* foot. What was what?"

"Are you sure you mean my left foot? That *flumpety flumpety* noise."

"I don't hear anything. Yes. But not in front; in back—"

"It's getting louder. I'm going to end up facing in the wrong—"

"I believe I *do* hear something. It's going *flumpety flumpety...*"

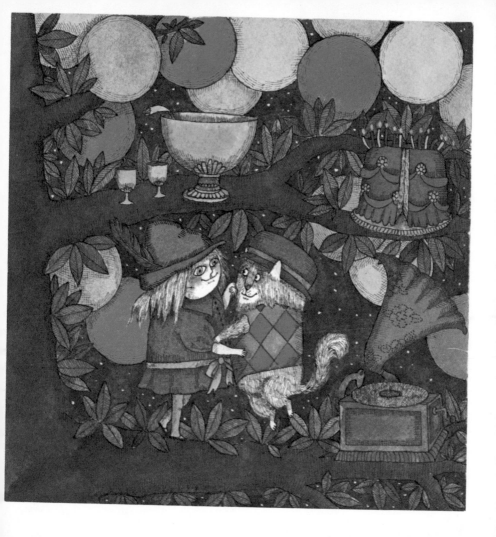

Just then a branch above their heads trembled slightly as something landed on it and a moment later a large, brightly colored moth appeared among the leaves and looked down at them.

"Oh, we have a guest," said Zenobia. "How delightful!"

"It's a party," said Fletcher, "with dancing and refreshments. Would you like to come to it?"

"How kind of you to invite me!" said the moth and flew down in a graceful semicircle to join them.

In a twinkling he drained the cup of punch Fletcher handed him and asked Zenobia to dance. Fletcher rewound the gramophone and off they went. Zenobia was surprised to find how tall the moth was when he stood up. When the record came to an end, Fletcher refilled everybody's cup.

Fletcher and Zenobia waltzed again; after several more false attempts, Fletcher at last succeeded in mastering the reverse. The moth, meanwhile, had a large dish of ice cream, and after that, a second, even larger.

Fletcher put a new needle in the gramophone and Zenobia and the moth danced a second time. Whether it was the dazzling combination of candle-light and moonlight or what, to Zenobia he really seemed taller than he had a few minutes ago.

Fletcher and Zenobia waltzed a third time: Fletcher's reverses were now absolutely brilliant and they both got quite giddy from doing them so often. The moth applauded each time in between bites of an enormous piece of cake.

Once more Zenobia and the moth danced to-gether. Although it was getting late and she had been dancing since the party began, she felt sure the moth was now taller than ever. Fletcher began to yawn behind the gramophone horn.

While the moth, at their insistence, was finishing what was left of the refreshments, Fletcher and Zenobia one by one untied the balloons and watched them float away on the gentle breeze.

"Wouldn't it be lovely," said Zenobia drowsily, "if we could just float away from the tree that way too?"

"How true!" said Fletcher, whose eyes were closing.

As they fell asleep, they could hear the moth crunching away on the last of the walnuts.

In the morning when Zenobia woke up, she gave a small scream. She was looking at a bewildering arrangement of large colored spots. What could they be? "Fletcher! Fletcher!" she cried. "Something has happened, but I don't know what."

A familiar face suddenly appeared at the edge of the spots. "It's his wings," said Fletcher in a whisper. "He's grown in the night. He's now perfectly enormous."

"I *thought* that was what was happening all along," said Zenobia, "but it seemed so unlikely. Of course, the cake was frightfully rich. All those eggs! All that butter and sugar!"

"And all that cream!" said Fletcher. "What beautiful spots!"

At that the moth woke up and stretched his feelers. "Good morning!"

"Good morning," said Fletcher and Zenobia.

"What a lovely party that was! Thank you so much for having me. I don't know when I've eaten quite so much."

"We're glad you liked it," said Zenobia.

"You've grown," said Fletcher.

The moth looked up at his wings. "So I have. It will be days of just nibbling before I get back to my proper size. Ah well, that's what parties are!"

The moth looked about him. "Do you live in this tree? It's a delightful place for a party, but what do you do when there isn't one?"

Fletcher explained their predicament.

"Oh, but I could easily carry you away on my back," said the moth. "That is, if you would care to come."

"It's our fondest wish," said Fletcher and Zenobia joyfully.

"Shall we be off, then?" said the moth.

They waited only long enough to gather up all the hats and to put on goggles to protect them against the wind (there was a third pair for the moth, who was terribly pleased), before settling themselves on the moth's back. He fanned his great wings several times and then they were no longer in the tree.

C683473

And so Fletcher and Zenobia flew away to the great world—and who knew what splendid occasions?

1796